Put Beginning Readers on the Right Track with
ALL ABOARD READING™

The All Aboard Reading series is especially designed for beginning readers. Written by noted authors and illustrated in full color, these are books that children really want to read—books to excite their imagination, expand their interests, make them laugh, and support their feelings. With fiction and nonfiction stories that are high interest and curriculum-related, All Aboard Reading books offer something for every young reader. And with four different reading levels, the All Aboard Reading series lets you choose which books are most appropriate for your children and their growing abilities.

Picture Readers
Picture Readers have super-simple texts, with many nouns appearing as rebus pictures. At the end of each book are 24 flash cards—on one side is a rebus picture; on the other side is the written-out word.

Station Stop 1
Station Stop 1 books are best for children who have just begun to read. Simple words and big type make these early reading experiences more comfortable. Picture clues help children to figure out the words on the page. Lots of repetition throughout the text helps children to predict the next word or phrase—an essential step in developing word recognition.

Station Stop 2
Station Stop 2 books are written specifically for children who are reading with help. Short sentences make it easier for early readers to understand what they are reading. Simple plots and simple dialogue help children with reading comprehension.

Station Stop 3
Station Stop 3 books are perfect for children who are reading alone. With longer text and harder words, these books appeal to children who have mastered basic reading skills. More complex stories captivate children who are ready for more challenging books.

In addition to All Aboard Reading books, look for All Aboard Math Readers™ (fiction stories that teach math concepts children are learning in school); All Aboard Science Readers™ (nonfiction books that explore the most fascinating science topics in age-appropriate language); and All Aboard Poetry Readers™ (funny, rhyming poems for readers of all levels).

All Aboard for happy reading!

Visit www.strawberryshortcake.com to join the Friendship Club and redeem your Strawberry Shortcake Berry Points for "berry" fun stuff!

Strawberry Shortcake™ © 2004 by Those Characters From Cleveland, Inc. Used under license by Penguin Young Readers Group. All rights reserved. Published by Grosset & Dunlap, a division of Penguin Young Readers Group, 345 Hudson Street, New York, New York 10014. ALL ABOARD READING and GROSSET & DUNLAP are trademarks of Penguin Group (USA) Inc. Printed in the U.S.A.

Library of Congress Cataloging-in-Publication Data

Bryant, Megan E.
  Strawberry Shortcake's filly friends / by Megan E. Bryant ; illustrated by SI Artists.
    p. cm. — (All aboard reading. Station stop 1)
  "Strawberry Shortcake."
  Summary: Strawberry Shortcake spends the day on Ice Cream Island with her friends and their Strawberryland Fillies.
  ISBN 0-448-43574-8 (pbk.)
  [1. Horses—Fiction. 2. Horsemanship—Fiction.] I. S.I. Artists (Group) II. Title. III. Series.
  PZ7.B826

2004000175

10   9   8   7   6   5   4   3   2   1

Strawberry Shortcake's Filly Friends

By Megan E. Bryant
Illustrated by SI Artists

Grosset & Dunlap • New York

Strawberry Shortcake is going to Ice Cream Island.

Strawberry Shortcake is going
to see her filly friends!

Angel Cake,
Ginger Snap,
Orange Blossom,
Blueberry Muffin,
and Honey Pie Pony
are going to
Ice Cream Island, too.

This will be a berry fun day!

Look!
There is
Ice Cream Island!

Look!

There are the fillies!

Honey Pie Pony is
Strawberry Shortcake's
filly friend.

Honey Pie Pony loves
to tell stories.

Milkshake is
Angel Cake's filly friend.

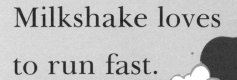

Milkshake loves
to run fast.

Blueberry Sundae is
Blueberry Muffin's filly friend.

Blueberry Sundae loves
to wear ribbons.

Cookie Dough is

Ginger Snap's filly friend.

16

Cookie Dough loves

to jump.

Orange Twist is
Orange Blossom's filly friend.

Orange Twist loves
to do tricks.

The girls go for a ride
with the fillies.

The girls brush
the fillies.

Berry pretty!

The girls share
a snack with the fillies.
Girls <u>and</u> fillies like
carrots and apples!

The girls have a treat
for the fillies—
sugar cubes!

The fillies have a treat
for the girls—
ice cream!

It is getting late.

It is time to go home.

The girls tuck
in the fillies.

They take good care
of their filly friends.

Good-bye, fillies!
See you next time.